Blue Sky
STUDIOS

# THE PEANUTS MOVIE

*by Schulz*

# The Sky's the Limit, Snoopy!

based on the *Peanuts* comic strip by Charles M. Schulz

adapted by Natalie Shaw

SIMON SPOTLIGHT
An imprint of Simon & Schuster Children's Publishing Division
New York   London   Toronto   Sydney   New Delhi
1230 Avenue of the Americas, New York, New York 10020
First Simon Spotlight paperback edition September 2015
© 2015 Peanuts Worldwide LLC. © 2015 Twentieth Century Fox Film Corporation.
All rights reserved, including the right of reproduction in whole or in part in any form.
SIMON SPOTLIGHT and colophon are registered trademarks of Simon & Schuster, Inc.
For information about special discounts for bulk purchases, please contact Simon & Schuster
Special Sales at 1-866-506-1949 or business@simonandschuster.com.
Manufactured in the United States of America   0815 NGS
2  4  6  8  10  9  7  5  3  1
ISBN 978-1-4814-4376-0
ISBN 978-1-4814-4377-7 (eBook)

Snoopy loves being Charlie Brown's dog, and Charlie Brown loves being Snoopy's owner! But while Snoopy may *look* and sometimes even act like a regular dog—he wears a collar, lives for his mealtime, and has a doghouse— his larger-than-a-dog's-life imagination makes him unique!

Snoopy sometimes imagines he is a regular kid like Charlie Brown. When Charlie Brown goes to school, Snoopy wants to go too . . . and he goes to great lengths to get inside!

"You can't come to school, Snoopy," Charlie Brown tells him. "Now be a good dog and go home."

*But I want to go to school!* Snoopy thinks.

To get inside, Snoopy tries to dress the part of a student. He walks up to the front doors of the school with confidence.

*Perfect!* he thinks. But his disguise doesn't fool anyone . . . and the door slams in his face!

Next he tries sneaking into class by sliding in through the ceiling like a secret agent. He lands on an empty chair and gets to work, adding paper to a three-ring binder.

*Not bad,* he thinks . . . but then the binder rings snap shut on his paw, and he can't stifle a yelp.

Snoopy's cover is blown, and he is thrown out of class!
"No dogs in school!" Lucy yells after him.

*She doesn't have to rub it in,* he thinks from inside the
dark garbage bin . . . but Snoopy quickly finds a bright spot:
a working, perfect typewriter! When you have an imagination
like Snoopy's, you're not down for long!

With his new tool of the writer's trade, Snoopy's next adventure begins! He goes home to his doghouse and writes the first line of what he *knows* will be a great novel.

*It was the greatest story ever told . . . ,* he types. He imagines meeting the dog of his dreams, a poodle named Fifi with an imagination to rival his own!

That's when Snoopy imagines hearing the whir of the Red Baron's plane, and becomes the Flying Ace, a skilled pilot! He sneaks to his doghouse, trying not to be seen by the enemy.

This time the Red Baron has gone too far . . . he has taken Fifi! As the Flying Ace, Snoopy crawls over to his doghouse—which doubles as his plane—trying not to be noticed by the Red Baron and planning his rescue mission!

As the Flying Ace's trusty airplane mechanic, Woodstock has been working on some repairs. He tries to warn the Flying Ace that the plane isn't ready to fly . . .

. . . but the Flying Ace is in a race to the skies and won't listen! He takes off and spots the Red Baron's plane ahead, and follows it all the way to Paris! In an aerial chase, they zoom toward the city.

The Flying Ace gets closer, and closer, and closer to the Red Baron and flies his plane up the side of the Eiffel Tower!

But even *imaginary* planes can only do so much . . . and when the Flying Ace's plane approaches the top of the Eiffel Tower, flying straight up like a rocket ship, it malfunctions and takes a nosedive.

Snoopy is writing more of his epic story when Charlie Brown comes by. A little red-haired girl has just moved in to a house across the street and Charlie Brown wants to meet her.

*What's the problem?* Snoopy thinks, but he can tell Charlie Brown is nervous and vows to help his owner.

They head to the front of Charlie Brown's house to wait for the perfect moment to meet the Little Red-Haired Girl.

"It's times like this that you need your faithful friend," Charlie Brown says to Snoopy.

"There she is!" Charlie Brown says. "I can't believe I'm going to go over and talk to the Little Red-Haired Girl."

Snoopy tries to encourage Charlie Brown, but he's still too nervous!

Charlie Brown gets all the way to the front door of the Little Red-Haired Girl's house, flower in hand, nervous smile on his face.

Snoopy is so excited . . . but Charlie Brown can't go through with it!

*I tried,* Snoopy thinks. Even man's best friend can only do so much!

Snoopy is determined to help Charlie Brown. When Charlie Brown decides to learn to dance to impress the Little Red-Haired Girl, Snoopy steps in. After all, he's a dog who not only has a big imagination, but also many talents! He teaches Charlie Brown to dance, or tries to.

"One, two, three, four," Charlie Brown counts out loud, trying to move to the music.

But not everyone has Snoopy's twinkle toes! When he imagines he's Joe Cool, he has the moves!

Snoopy is a loyal friend to Sally, too. When she is practicing to be a rodeo star for the school talent show, Sally jumps on his back. He takes it in stride—after the initial wince! That's love!

Snoopy has a big imagination and talents galore, but he also knows what's really important. All he really needs to be happy is: a good meal with Charlie Brown, . . .

a friend like Woodstock to share his secrets and adventures, . . .

... and visions of rescuing a wonderful dog named Fifi, who he can share his dreams with! When Snoopy's imagination takes flight, the sky's the limit!